For Andrew, Christopher, and Joshua, who wake up every morning with the most terrific cowlicks—
and to their grandpa, who first observed that his boys had been visited by the Cowlick Fairy

—C.D.

A GOLDEN BOOK • NEW YORK

Copyright © 2007 by Christin Ditchfield. Illustrations copyright © 2007 by Rosalind Beardshaw.
All rights reserved. Published in the United States by Golden Books, an imprint of Random House Children's Books,
a division of Random House, Inc., New York. GOLDEN BOOKS, A GOLDEN BOOK, the G colophon, and the distinctive
gold spine are registered trademarks of Random House, Inc.
www.goldenbooks.com
www.randomhouse.com/kids
Educators and librarians, for a variety of teaching tools, visit us at
www.randomhouse.com/teachers
ISBN: 978-0-375-83540-7
Library of Congress Control Number: 2005931763
PRINTED IN MALAYSIA
10 9 8 7 6 5 4 3 2 1
First Edition

COWLICK!

By Christin Ditchfield

Illustrated by Rosalind Beardshaw

 A GOLDEN BOOK • NEW YORK

When the moon rises high
and the stars shine bright

Little boys in bed with their eyes shut tight

Clip-clop, clip-clop down the hall
Funny shadow on the wall

Closer now—tiptoe, tiptoe
Doorknob turning very slow

To the bedside she comes sneaking

Lifting covers, gently peeking

Sees a face so soft and sweet
Framed with hair so smooth and neat

Quickly, as he starts to stir,
Before he wakes and catches her,

Bending low, bestows a kiss:

Sluuurrpp!

Sluuurrpp!

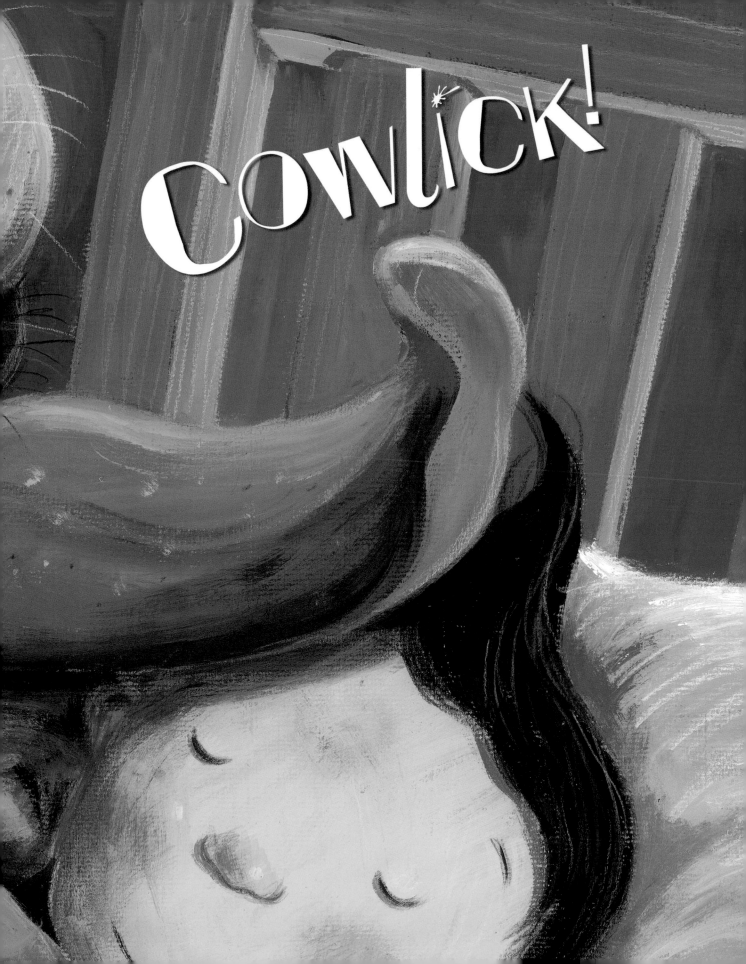

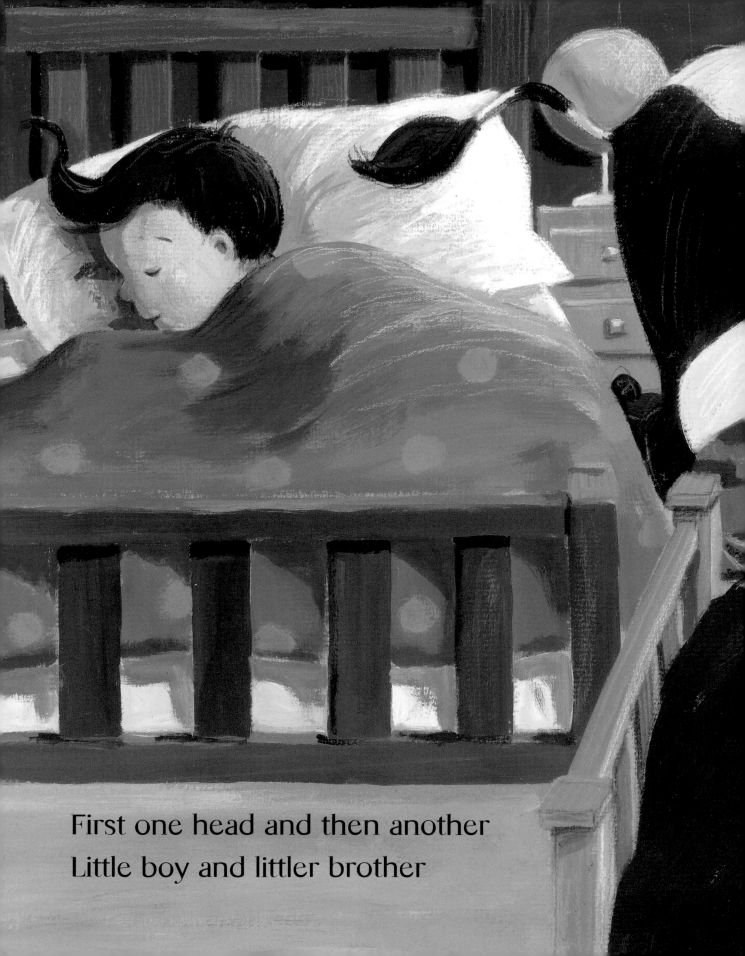

First one head and then another
Little boy and littler brother

Her eyes a-twinkle, she's had her fun
She slips away before the sun

"Breakfast time! Get out of bed!
What has happened to your head?"

Bathroom mirror shows it all

Once-flat hair now standing tall

No brush or comb
will do the trick

When you've been given a big cowlick!